The Golden Key

This

The
a fur ɔrian stories linking with the History
National Curriculum.

Franklin Watts Australia
Level 17/207 Kent Street
Sydney NSW 2000

Series editor: Paula Borton
Consultant: Joan Blyth
Designer: Kirstie Billingham

A CIP catalogue record for this book
is available from the British Library.

ISBN: 978 0 7496 8509 6

Dewey Classification: 941.081

Printed in Great Britain by CPI Cox & Wyman, Reading, RG1 8EX

Franklin Watts is a division of Hachette Children's Books,
an Hachette Livre UK company.
www.hachettelivre.co.uk

The Golden Key

by
Mary Hooper

Illustrations by Lesley Bisseker

FRANKLIN WATTS
LONDON•SYDNEY

Ma

Pa

Poppy

Alfred

George

Marigold

Lily and Rose

Daisy

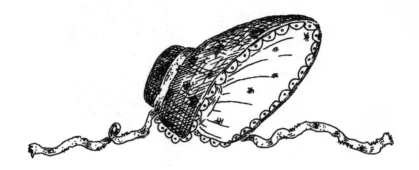

1

Life Can be Tough!

Poppy sighed. "Oh, Ma. Do we have to go to school?"

Ma nodded. "There's no stone-picking in the fields – the farmer hasn't sent for us. You'd best go to school while you can."

"We don't learn anything there,"

Poppy said. "All we do is sit in the room
and..." But Poppy's Ma had jumped up
and made a run to catch the baby, who'd
lurched over to the ladder in the corner of
the cottage and was trying to climb it.

That morning the Harding family had
been up early, as usual, and by six o'clock
everyone had splashed their faces and
made a visit to the bucket which stood in a
tin shed near their cottage.

Poppy was the oldest child, so she'd been allowed to use the washing water first (after Ma and Dad, of course) and then, in turn, it had been used by Alfred and George and then the girls – twins Lily and Rose, then Marigold. No one had bothered much with washing baby Daisy, which was just as well, for the water was grey and murky by the time it was her turn. Mrs Harding was expecting her eighth child, but she hadn't told anyone yet. For one thing she thought it was another girl and she'd run out of flower names, and for another the family were finding it hard enough to feed seven.

Poppy's dad,

who was a farm hand, had gone off to work with Alfred and George, leaving the girls trying to get out of going to school.

"There's really not much point in going," Poppy tried again with Ma. "And anyway, Old Mother Wood said we're not to come to school without boots and I haven't got any."

Her mother tutted. "You get into school sharp and she won't even notice."

Poppy pulled a face. School was boring. If it was arithmetic it was sitting in rows chanting tables, if it was English it was sitting in rows chanting poems.

"Are we all going?" she asked.

Ma nodded. She put Daisy down onto the floor of the cottage. The baby crawled away towards the open door, not seeming to mind the hard bricks under her knees and toes. "Best go when you can," Ma repeated. "While there's pennies to pay for you. You'll be leaving school soon enough, anyway. Cut some bread to take for your dinner, will you?"

Poppy cut some hunks of bread to take to school, spreading them with lard and sprinkling them with salt and pepper.

Sometimes, in the autumn, Ma bought some sugar and made jam from the blackberries, but at this time of the year there was nothing but lard.

Poppy went up the ladder to the bedroom to look for everyone's school smocks. It was several weeks since they'd been to school. Last week they'd all been stone-picking on the farm, before that she'd gone bird-scaring with her brothers, and then, for two weeks, she'd been out with Ma, helping with the laundry at the big house.

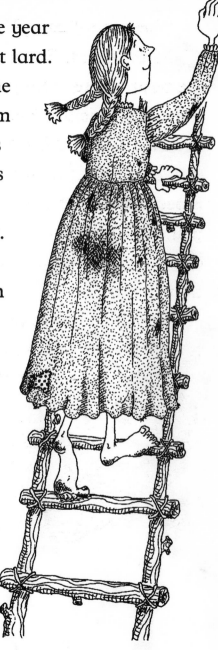

Her own smock was creased and grubby, but she put it on and smoothed it out as best she could. She started looking for her bonnet. She could go without shoes, she could even go without a smock, but since the sun had started shining she wouldn't go out without her bonnet. Sun meant freckles and she hated freckles.

She went downstairs and looked suspiciously at the twins, giggling in the corner. "Have you hidden my bonnet again?" she asked sternly.

"Marigold had it!" Lily said and Poppy ran outside to look for Marigold, who'd gone into the yard to play with the baby.

Marigold had put Poppy's bonnet on the baby's head. She'd put it on backwards, though, and the baby was screaming.

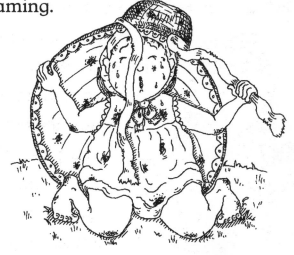

"You're not to take my bonnet!" Poppy said crossly to Marigold, and she snatched it off and put it on, tying the ribbons tightly under her chin.

Rose came up behind her. "Mind the sun don't get you!"

"Careful you don't get any more freckles!" said Lily.

"I see a new one coming now!" teased Rose.

Poppy marched indoors.

"Freckly! Speckly! Ginger checkly!" Lily called, and although the words didn't make sense, she and Rose burst into giggles.

"Freckly! Speckly! Ginger checkly!" they chanted after Poppy as she stormed into the cottage.

2

A Mysterious Visitor

Poppy's ma was collecting the breakfast plates ready to take outside and rinse in the remains of the washing water.

"Don't mind the little ones," she said to Poppy. "They're just jealous."

"Jealous of these?" Poppy muttered.

Of all the children, she was the only one with ginger hair and freckles. She tugged at the long plaits which hung over her shoulder. "I wish my hair was their colour..."

"You just wait," said her mother. "You're special. Chosen."

"So you keep telling me," said Poppy. She'd been born shortly after Queen Victoria had come to the throne and Ma had wanted to name her Victoria, after the new queen.

When her Dad had seen
her, though, he said
any girl with hair that
red was a Poppy,
and the name
had stuck.

Ma went
outside to the
yard with the
plates and Poppy
reached up to the
mantlepiece to take down the locket which
was hidden there.

The locket was the only thing the
Harding family had which was of any
value. Ma's family had been rich once, so
she often told them, but then their money
had mysteriously disappeared and the only
thing left to show for it was the locket.

It was an oval shape, large and golden. Inside there was a gold key, and some writing. Poppy could only read one or two words of this and didn't think it sounded very interesting, all she wanted to do was open the locket and look at her freckles in the polished surface.

She stared down at her nose, muttering under her breath. Although none of the family could read properly, Poppy's dad had taught her numbers.

"Fourteen!" she gasped when she'd finished. One more freckle since yesterday! Now it was sunny they just seemed to multiply. At this rate, she thought, they'd all join up and then her skin would be the same colour as her hair, and people in the village would laugh at her and...

"Poppy!" Ma shouted from outside.

"Find everyone's slates and then get Marigold ready for school!" Poppy sighed and put the locket back on the shelf. It took nearly an hour to walk to school and, once the bell had rung at nine o'clock, Old Ma Wood would stand at the door swishing her cane ready to use it on anyone who was late.

School was in the nearby town, and
was run from Old Ma Wood's sitting
room. Poppy had heard that there would
be a proper school built soon, with
classrooms and desks, but she knew it
would never be ready in time for her. Most
children had left school by the time they
were ten, anyway.

There were twenty-eight children in
Old Ma Wood's sitting room that morning
– mostly girls,
because many of
the boys
were
working in
the fields.
The room
was crowded
and stuffy and
Poppy, who was
the biggest there,
was ordered to
look after the
younger
children while
they did their
numbers.

"Where's your boots?" Old Ma Wood asked Poppy sharply as the four sisters went in.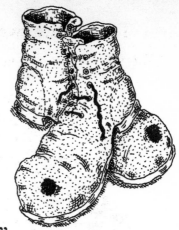

"Outgrown them, Ma'am," Poppy said.

"You know the rules!" Old Ma Wood snapped.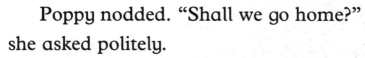

Poppy nodded. "Shall we go home?" she asked politely.

Old Ma Wood pursed her lips. "I'll overlook it this once," she said, "but you must tell your mother to apply to the poor box. I believe the squire's daughter has donated some of her old boots."

"Very well, Ma'am," Poppy said, pulling a face as she turned her back. She'd known she wouldn't be made to go

home, for if Old Ma Wood turned Poppy away then Rose and Lily and Marigold would go too, and then she wouldn't get their two pence a week for school fees.

In a corner of the room, Poppy struggled to keep order.

The older children were chanting a daffodil poem over and over again and some of the others were shouting out their six times table.

Old Ma Wood had slipped away for what she called 'a morsel of refreshment',

and Poppy could see her through a window in the sitting room door, sharing a plate of cakes with the vicar in the kitchen.

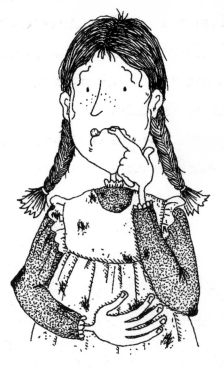

"Cakes!" Poppy thought, and she looked enviously through the window again. Raisin cakes and chocolate cakes and some with shiny cherries on the top. She licked her lips...it had been ages since she'd had a cake - since the Sunday school outing last August.

While Poppy was staring longingly,

there was a noise outside and one of the boys suddenly shouted, "A carriage! A big gold carriage coming by!"

Poppy ran to the window and looked out. Sure enough, a magnificent carriage was coming down the road, pulled by four horses with plumes.

"Quick, children!" Poppy said excitedly. "Outside!" And she ushered the children out just in time. The boys made hasty bows and the girls bobbed a curtsy – for it was certainly someone important – and Old Ma Wood and the Vicar ran outside to gawp at the size and the elegance of the carriage. While everyone was talking and looking, Poppy managed to get back inside first and, almost scared to death at her own daring,

picked a cherry off the top of one of the small cakes and popped it into her mouth.

At least she'd got something out of school that day she thought on the way home.

3

Bad News!

It didn't take long for Poppy to find out who'd been in the fine carriage that had passed the school that day.

When they arrived home from school, they found their dad sitting outside the cottage, his face grey. This was strange and unusual – Poppy had never before known her dad to have a day off work in the week, and he was never ill.

The girls clustered round him. Beside him on the wooden bench were Alfred and George, looking scared.

"What's happened?" Poppy asked. "Have they given you a day's holiday?" Her dad shook his head. "A lifetime holiday," he muttered.

"What's that mean?" Poppy asked.

"Leave your dad alone!" Ma called sharply from inside the cottage. "You'll find out what's up soon enough."

Daisy, who'd been sitting on a scrubby patch of grass near the door, sensed that something was wrong and began to cry. This set Marigold off.

"Sssh!" Poppy said, and she picked up both Daisy and Marigold and beckoned to the boys to come away.

All seven children went round the back
of the cottage - to the little wooden shack
where, in better times, they'd kept a pig.

"Now, what is it?" Poppy asked Alfie, who was six years old and could usually be relied on to be sensible. "What happened?"

Alfie shook his head. "Dunno," he said. "A big carriage arrived up at the Hall, then Dad was sent for by the guv'nor and when he came back he said we were going home. George was plucking turkeys and I had to go and get him. And then we walked all the way home and Dad didn't speak."

Rose, too, began to cry at the strangeness of it all. Poppy glared at the smaller ones. "If you all be quiet I might be able to hear what's going on," she said, and she put Daisy down and crept to the side of the cottage to listen.

But when she found out what had happened, Poppy felt like crying herself.

"Dad's lost his job!" she reported back to the scared children. "So have Alfie and George. The farm's been bought by a rich lord and he's bringing his own men in."

"But what will happen?" Rose whimpered.

Poppy shook her head. "I don't know." As the wails started again she added quickly, "I expect Dad will get another job soon enough."

But Poppy knew that was far from certain – and she hadn't told them the worst bit – that their cottage went with the job. If Dad lost his job then they lost the cottage as well.

"They'll let us stay for three months," she had overheard her dad saying, "then we'll have to get out."

"What if you haven't found a job by then?" Ma had cried in alarm.

"The workhouse," Dad had said flatly, and then Poppy had crept away.

Poppy lay awake that night, listening to the fitful breathing of her brothers and sisters and the low murmur of Ma and Dad talking behind the old curtain that divided the bedroom.

She knew the workhouse, it was a big ugly-looking building in the next town. Once, when she and Alfie had gone on an errand for Ma, she'd stood on Alfie's back to look through the windows.

"What can you see?" Alfie had asked, too scared to look through himself. "Are there people in there to beat you? Are there chains and wicked ghosties?"

"Of course not," Poppy called down. "It's just a great big room with rows of

people having their dinner."

But she'd shivered as she said it, for the ward she was looking into contained benches with rows and rows of thin, hopeless-looking women seated on them. All were dressed the same, all looked worn and beaten.

"Are there any children?" Alfie had asked. "I heard that children have to go into a workhouse if their fathers die."

Poppy had shaken her head. "There are no children here – they split up families. The children and the men will be in other buildings."

Alfie had given a whimper. "Come on, Poppy! They might come out and get us!"

So Poppy had jumped down and they'd gone home. It had only been a quick glimpse, but now Poppy strained to remember every detail of the dismal place, going over and over them in her head as she tossed and turned on the straw. Oh, what if they ended up there?

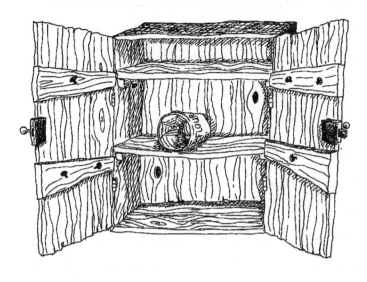

4

The Golden Locket

"It's no good," Ma said, sitting down
heavily on the kitchen stool. "There's not
a morsel left – not a crumb of bread, not a
grain of flour. Not even a penny-piece to
buy milk for Daisy."

"There's the money I earn at Old Ma

Wood's," Poppy said. The girls had, of course, stopped going to school when Dad had lost his job, but Poppy had managed to get a job cleaning the schoolroom six nights a week.

"You won't get that until Saturday," said Ma. "We'll be starved by then."

"Perhaps Dad will send word..." Poppy said, but there wasn't much hope in her voice. Dad had been gone for five weeks now. He was travelling from town to town trying to get a job. "Perhaps the vicar will have some news for us," she added.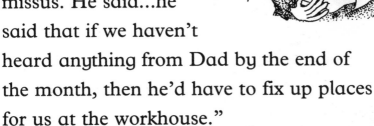

Ma shook her head. "I saw him yesterday when I went to beg a potato from his missus. He said...he said that if we haven't heard anything from Dad by the end of the month, then he'd have to fix up places for us at the workhouse."

Poppy felt tears spring to her eyes. "Oh, Ma!"

"If we could just keep going a while longer," Ma said. "I'm sure your dad will find something. Or maybe the vicar's wife will hear of a job in service for you."

Poppy wiped her eyes with the back of

her hand. "Alfie and George have gone out poaching. Maybe they'll bring back a rabbit. And me and the twins will have a hunt around in the fields for early green stuff."

"And there's the locket!" Ma suddenly exclaimed. "We can pawn that and use the money to buy food!"

Poppy's face brightened. "Is it worth a lot?"

"Enough to keep us going for a week or two," Ma said, and she got up and took the locket from the mantlepiece.

"I'll take it for you!" Poppy said eagerly. "I'll take it and tell the old pawnbroker that we want as much money for it as we can get."

"Only pawn it, mind," Ma said. "Don't sell it. I want to have it back someday." She pushed the little catch and

the locket swung open. "I want it back just in case it leads us to the treasure!"

Poppy looked over her shoulder at the inscription. "Tell me the story again – I've forgotten it."

"Well," Ma said, "Great-Gran had four children – two boys and two girls. They were a very well-to-do family, but one day there was a big argument and they all fell out. The brothers and sisters never spoke again, and Great-Gran was so angry with them that when she died she ordered someone to hide all her money."

"And her children didn't get any of it?"

"All they got was one piece of jewellery each. The boys got pocket watches and the girls got lockets, each with a four-leafed clover engraved outside and one line of a riddle within. If they got together and made up, they could solve the riddle and find the money – but they never did."

"What does the line on our locket say?" Poppy asked.

"*When life's torch flames burn no more*," said Ma, touching each of the words in turn with her finger.

"What does that mean?"

"No idea," Ma shrugged. "And my own Ma didn't know, either."

She handed the locket to Poppy. "But before it goes to the pawnbroker you'd best note those words down..."

So Poppy did, borrowing a pen and a small piece of paper from the schoolroom that evening and copying the words carefully. She didn't think she'd be able to find the other three pieces of jewellery and solve the riddle, but – well, just in case. And when the town's pawnbroker handed over a golden guinea to Poppy for the locket and said that he had no use for the key, she hung it round her neck on a piece of string. This was just in case, too.

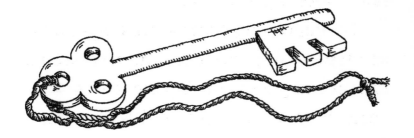

5

A Job for Poppy

Pawning the locket bought the Harding family enough food for nearly three weeks. And before the three weeks were up, two other things happened.

It was Friday and Old Ma Wood's school was over for the week. Poppy,

working as usual, had moved all the chairs
into the middle of the room, ready to scrub
the floorboards around them, when Old
Ma Wood bustled through from the
kitchen, her face red with excitement.

"I never did! Such an honour!" she
said. "The vicar has
just sent to say that
Lady Throckmorten
and her daughter
are calling
on me!"

"Shall I put everything neat again, then?" Poppy asked, catching some of the excitement and thinking that she'd never seen a real lady, close-up before.

"No time, no time!" Old Ma Wood flapped. "Just get in the kitchen and make yourself scarce, girl!"

Poppy did as she was told, making sure she got herself a good viewing point through the kitchen window.

It had been the Throckmortens who had caused Dad to lose his job, so she wanted to have a good look at them.

"Whatever can they want? Oh, don't tell me that the daughter is going to join my school!" Old Ma Wood said as she ran back into the kitchen to change her apron and put on a fresh cap.

There was the sound of a carriage and horses drawing up in the lane outside, and Old Ma Wood adjusted her cap and dashed to the door, where Poppy saw her curtsy deeply. "Do enter...I'm most honoured," she said, and there was a murmur in reply.

Footsteps came through to the school room. "To think that such a great lady would think of sending her dear daughter to my humble school," Poppy heard.

"My dear woman!" came the reply. "My precious Isabella has a governess. We wouldn't think of sending her to a village school."

"No, no. Of course not. My mistake," Old Ma Wood blustered.

"Just a visit...how kind...most honoured."

"I've come because we have a vacancy for a scullery maid in our household," went on the refined voice. She moved further into the schoolroom and Poppy, standing well back in the kitchen, widened her eyes at the richness of the ruffled silk gown the woman wore. "We were hoping you might recommend one of your older girls for the position."

"I'm afraid school is over for this week, Ma'am," Old Ma Wood said. "On Monday, though, I shall select some girls and send them for your kind approval."

"Next week will be too late," came the reply. "The whole household, apart from my husband and his manservants, departs for our London home first thing Monday morning."

"There's one here, Mama!" came a piercing voice, and Poppy, who'd been pretending to dust, looked up to see a girl about her own age pointing at her.

Lady Throckmorten swayed across the floor so that she could have a good look at Poppy. "Come out, girl," she said. "Let's see the size of you."

"This is Poppy Harding," Old Ma Wood said. And she murmured something which Poppy couldn't catch.

Poppy came out and she and Isabella stared at each other. They were the same age and height, but there the likeness

ended. Isabella was plump, and wearing a cream satin dress. She had shiny, curly hair and pink cheeks. Poppy was thin and pale where she wasn't freckled, and wore her usual rough cotton dress with a smock over the top. She'd managed to get some boots but these were fourth-hand and well-worn.

"What an ill-dressed child – and what vulgar colour hair!" Lady Throckmorten said, looking down her nose at Poppy.

"Oh, she'll do!" said Isabella rudely, and she turned away. "Can we go home now, Mother? I'm bored."

"Yes, I suppose she'll do," said Lady Throckmorten after studying Poppy a moment longer. "She looks strong enough – and I promised the vicar I'd take a girl from the village."

She began to walk from the room. "Poppy Harding, you're hired! Come up to the Hall tomorrow morning and see the housekeeper," she commanded. "She'll give you a uniform and tell you about wages. You'll be sharing a room with the kitchen maid."

Poppy blinked in amazement. A job! A proper job! And fancy sharing a room with just one other person!

Old Ma Wood nudged her violently, Poppy remembered her manners and dipped a curtsy. "Thank you very much, Ma'am. I do hope I suit you," she said with only the faintest trace of scorn.

"Just think!" she said to Ma when she got home. "A real proper live-in job in a big house in London! And I'll only have one other person in my bedroom!"

"Imagine!" Ma marvelled. She gave her a rare hug. "I'll miss you, ducks, but it'll be one less mouth to feed. And with a new baby coming along in the autumn..."

"Oh, not another, Ma!" Poppy said.

"We'll manage. And now you're in

service you'll be able to send a bit of money home."

"Of course I will," Poppy promised.

"And what do you think?" Ma added, smiling broadly, "the vicar sent his boy to say that he's had a message from Morchester. Your dad's living there, he's got a job on the railways and he's sending for all of us as soon as he can!"

Poppy hugged her mum back, happy that her dad had got a job and even happier that no one would be going into a workhouse. She would try very hard not to cry about leaving home, she decided, for she was really very grown up now. When she saw her family again, though, it would be at a new house, in a new town and everything would be different.

Feeling a bit shaky with all the

excitement, she began looking round for a paper bag in which to pack the few bits and pieces of clothing she owned. Her life in the country and her childhood were both over and done with. London, she knew, would be a whole new life.

Victorian Life

Children at work

Country children were expected to start working on the land at a very young age. Children like Poppy and her brothers and sisters would have worked as bird scarers, scaring the birds away from newly sown crops, or picking the stones out of ploughed fields before planting the seeds, or picking and sorting potatoes. And everyone, including the little toddlers, would have to help stack the corn at harvest time. Families would often have over ten children so they would have more to send out to work and earn wages.

The family home

Poor people often lived in little more than a tumbledown shed, with one room upstairs and one room down. It was usually small, damp and would have had hardly any furniture – none of the children would have had chairs of their own. Upstairs was just a shelf reached by a ladder. If there was a lavatory, it was outside and would be just a bucket or a big hole in the ground. Dirt would be thrown down the hole every evening.

Country schools

These were sometimes known as 'Dame Schools' and run by old women with little or no education. Sometimes the basic rules of reading and

writing would be taught, and the vicar's daughter
might come in now and again to teach the girls
sewing, but the 'Dames' were often no more than
child-minders.

The workhouse

Workhouses were a bit like prisons for people who
could not get jobs. Families were separated and
children only allowed to see their mothers for
a short time each day. Everyone had to wear a
uniform. There was not much to eat and they had
to do horrible jobs that no one else wanted.
They were so bad
that some people
would rather
starve to
death than
go in one.